© Joshua McManus 2016

I'm mad about pizza, isn't that neat? A pizza a day is what I eat.

A pizza with cheese while in the bath,
I am not joking nor having a laugh.

A pizza with ham, isn't that great?
When eating it quietly,
staying up late.

A pizza with mushroom, yes all for me!
And a slice in my pocket while
climbing a tree.

A pizza with pepperoni,
that is a long word!
But a slice was taken by a huge bird!

A pizza with chicken, I sure like to hog;
And a slice in my mouth while walking
the dog!

A pizza with sausage, wow how cool!
A slice in my mouth
as I bomb dive the pool.

A pizza with pineapple, oh what a pain;
Trying to eat while flying plane.

A pizza with salami, oh what a treat;
While drumming the sound of an
awesome beat!

A pizza with olives, that sounds okay;
While sailing a boat on a lovely day.

A pizza with bacon, wow how yum!
Sliding down stairs using my bum.

A pizza with peppers, a slice or two;
Scoffing it quickly while on the loo.

A pizza with fish, oh how delish;
I must tell the chef
what a wonderful dish.

A pizza with beef, that's enough said;
I caught it mid air
as I bounced off my bed.

A pizza with onions, I guess it was fine
As I dug a huge hole as big as a mine.

A pizza with steak, I sure did like;
Scoffing a slice while jumping my bike.

A pizza with garlic, please don't tell;
I grossed out the teacher with the smell

A pizza with meatballs,
I can't help but sing!
While gulping it quickly
going fast on a swing!

I am mad about pizza, it's no surprise;
I told you, I did, I tell no lies!

But wait a second, what is that?
Oh no! My tummy is SOOOOO

I didn't see my tummy grow;
It happened, quick I didn't know!

So be careful what you put in your tum,
You've only got the one.
Because if you get so big and fat It
really ain't no fun.

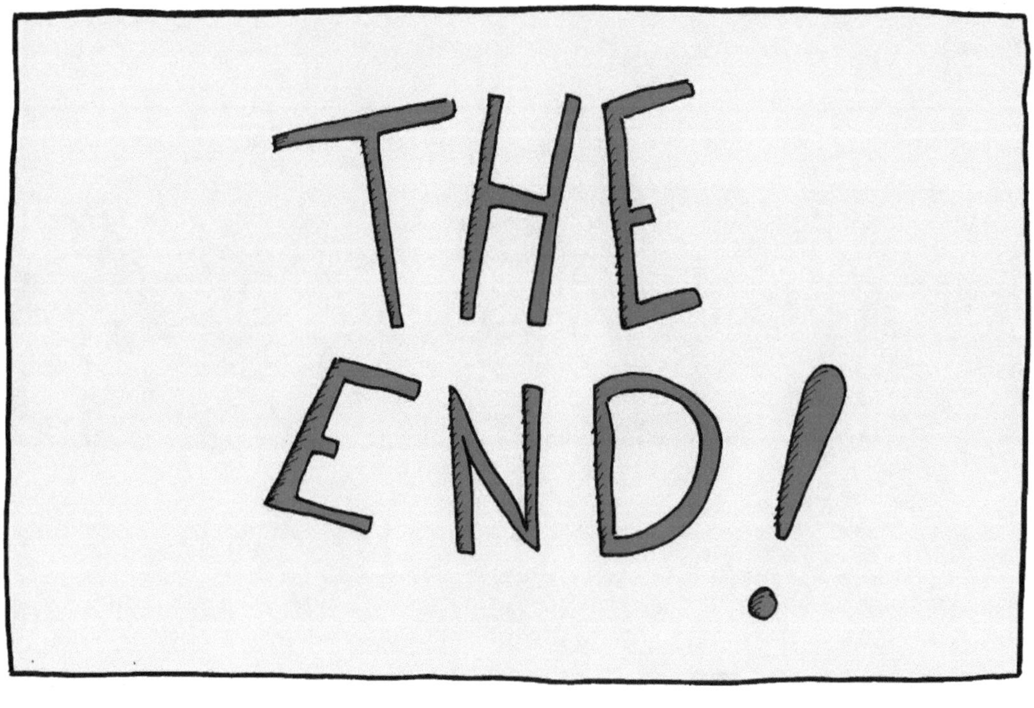
THE END!

CPSIA information can be obtained
at www.ICGtesting.com
Printed in the USA
BVIIW022039040719
552612BV00009B/67/P